# CHEVROLET CAMARO Z28

BY EMILY ROSE OACHS

BELLWETHER MEDIA • MINNEAPOLIS, MN

Are you ready to take it to the extreme? Torque books thrust you into the action-packed world of sports, vehicles, mystery, and adventure. These books may include dirt, smoke, fire, and dangerous stunts.

**WARNING**: read at your own risk.

This edition first published in 2017 by Bellwether Media, Inc.



Library of Congress Cataloging-in-Publication Data

Names: Oachs, Emily Rose, author.
Title: Chevrolet Camaro Z28 / by Emily Rose Oachs.
Other titles: Car Crazy (Minneapolis, Minn.)
Description: Minneapolis, MN : Bellwether Media, Inc., 2017. | Series: Torque: Car Crazy | Audience: Ages 7-12. | Includes bibliographical references and index.
Identifiers: LCCN 2016034504 (print) | LCCN 2016036393 (ebook) | ISBN 9781626175761 (hardcover : alk. paper) | ISBN 9781681033051 (ebook)
Subjects: LCSH: Camaro automobile–Juvenile literature.
Classification: LCC TL215.C33 O23 2017 (print) | LCC TL215.C33 (ebook) | DDC 629.222/2–dc23
LC record available at https://lccn.loc.gov/2016034504



Editor: Betsy Rathburn Designer: Brittany McIntosh

Printed in the United States of America, North Mankato, MN.

# TABLE OF CONTENTS

# TRACK STAR

A driver climbs into a Chevrolet Camaro Z28. He buckles his seat belt and revs the engine. The sports car roars out onto the track.

No other cars are around. The Z28 lets loose. It hugs tight curves and speeds down **straightaways**.

Wind beats at the windshield, but the Camaro Z28 does not slow down. The driver pushes the car past 150 miles (241 kilometers) per hour.

The car finishes the loop and continues on for a second lap. Nothing can stop the Camaro Z28!

# THE HISTORY OF CHEVROLET

Louis Chevrolet

William C. Durant

Louis Chevrolet was a record-setting car racer during the early 1900s. In 1911, he went into business with William C. Durant, the founder of General Motors. They started the Chevrolet Motor Company. They believed Louis's racing fame would help sell their cars.

Their first automobile was an expensive **luxury** car. But soon the company began making more affordable cars. They were priced lower than the competition to sell more.

Louis Chevrolet in the 1910s

## BEST-DRESSED DESIGN

THE CHEVROLET LOGO WAS FIRST USED IN THE 1910S. ITS SHAPE EARNED IT THE "CHEVROLET BOWTIE" NICKNAME!

1967 Chevrolet Camaro Z28

In 1918, the Chevrolet Motor Company officially joined General Motors. Soon, Chevrolet was among the country's top carmakers. Americans loved the sleek style, low prices, and high quality of Chevrolet cars.

The company went on to create some of America's best-known cars. In 1966, Chevrolet introduced the Camaro to the public. It made this car to compete with other **muscle cars**. Today, Chevrolet still makes some of the most popular cars in the country!

# CHEVROLET CAMARO Z28

The Chevrolet Camaro Z28 first hit roads in 1966. This version of the Camaro was designed to rule the racetrack.

**1967 Chevrolet Camaro Z28**

2015 Chevrolet Camaro Z28

In 2010, Chevrolet released the fifth **generation** of the Camaro Z28. Like earlier versions, the new Z28 is light and speedy. It can finish Germany's famous Nürburgring track in less than 8 minutes!

# TECHNOLOGY AND GEAR

Engineers made the fifth-generation Camaro Z28 more **aerodynamic** than ever before. Air moves quickly over its body thanks to its low, wide shape.

A front **splitter** and rear **spoiler** help the car stay in control. While driving fast, the car's strong, wide tires grip the road.

## ON THE BIG SCREEN

A 1967 CAMARO Z28 APPEARED IN THE 2015 MOVIE *FURIOUS 7*. THE CREW HAD FIVE OF THE CARS ON HAND FOR FILMING.

An **aluminum** and **carbon fiber** body makes the Camaro Z28 light and fast. A **V8 engine** powers this speedy car. On the hood, the **air extractor** cools the engine.

Five driving modes offer different levels of power and **handling**. These help the driver adjust to any road condition.

## KEEPING IT LIGHT

THE CAMARO Z28'S ENGINEERS WORKED HARD TO MAKE THE CAR AS LIGHT AS POSSIBLE. AS A RESULT, THE BASE MODEL COMES WITH ONLY ONE SPEAKER AND NO AIR CONDITIONING!

Inside, the Camaro Z28 feels like a race car. The short gear shifter lets the driver quickly change from one gear to the next. Thick cushions on the seats

# 2015 CHEVROLET CAMARO Z28 SPECIFICATIONS

| | |
|---|---|
| CAR STYLE | COUPE |
| ENGINE | 7.0L V8 |
| TOP SPEED | 172 MILES (277 KILOMETERS) PER HOUR |
| 0 - 60 TIME | 4.4 SECONDS |
| HORSEPOWER | 505 HP (376 KILOWATTS) @ 6,100 RPM |
| CURB WEIGHT | 3,820 POUNDS (1,733 KILOGRAMS) |
| WIDTH | 76.9 INCHES (195 CENTIMETERS) |
| LENGTH | 192.3 INCHES (488 CENTIMETERS) |
| HEIGHT | 52.4 INCHES (133 CENTIMETERS) |
| WHEEL SIZE | 19 INCHES (48 CENTIMETERS) |
| COST | STARTS AROUND $73,300 |

# TODAY AND THE FUTURE

The Camaro Z28's stripped-down design makes it a commanding competitor on the track. It can easily beat other cars. Even those with stronger engines have fallen to the Camaro Z28.

Chevrolet continues to improve the Z28 with every generation. This car will bring talent and speed to the racetrack for years to come!

## TOP CAR

IN 2015, THE Z28 WAS NAMED AN *AUTOMOBILE* ALL-STAR CAR OF THE YEAR BY *AUTOMOBILE* MAGAZINE!

2015 Chevrolet Camaro Z28

## HOW TO SPOT A CHEVROLET CAMARO Z28

FRONT SPLITTER

HOOD AIR EXTRACTOR

REAR SPOILER

# GLOSSARY

**aerodynamic**—having a shape that can move through the air quickly

**air extractor**—a part that draws cooler air toward the engine

**aluminum**—a strong, lightweight metal

**carbon fiber**—a strong, lightweight material made from woven pieces of carbon

**generation**—a version of the same model

**handling**—how a car performs around turns

**luxury**—expensive and offering great comfort

**muscle cars**—high-performance sports cars with strong engines

**splitter**—a flat scoop under the front bumper that makes a car more aerodynamic

**spoiler**—a part on the back of a car that helps the car grip the road

**straightaways**—straight parts of the track

**V8 engine**—an engine with 8 cylinders arranged in the shape of a "V"

# TO LEARN MORE

## AT THE LIBRARY

Gray, Leon. *Fast and Cool Cars*. New York, N.Y.: DK, Penguin Random House, 2015.

Kenney, Karen Latchana. *Thrilling Sports Cars*. North Mankato, Minn.: Capstone Press, 2015.

Quinlan, Julia J. *Corvette*. New York, N.Y.: PowerKids Press, 2013.

## ON THE WEB

Learning more about the Chevrolet Camaro Z28 is as easy as 1, 2, 3.

1. Go to www.factsurfer.com.

2. Enter "Chevrolet Camaro Z28" into the search box.

3. Click the "Surf" button and you will see a list of related web sites.

With factsurfer.com, finding more information is just a click away.

# INDEX




The images in this book are reproduced through the courtesy of: ilikewaffles11/ Flickr, front cover; General Motors, pp. 4-5, 6-7, 8 (left, right), 9 (bottom), 13, 14-15, 16 (top, bottom), 17, 18, 20-21, 21 (bottom right); Everett Collection/ Newscom, p. 9 (top); Ron Kimball/ KimballStock, pp. 10-11; StanRohrer, p. 12; REUTERS/ Alamy, p. 19; Kamal Aboul-Hosn/ Flickr, p. 21 (bottom left, bottom center).